TO MY DAUGHTERS - Thank you for the way you encourage me each day. I love you with all of my heart. I am so grateful for the way you continue to grow in your walk with the Lord.

MY HUSBAND, MIKE - Thank you for helping me in the pursuit of my dream. Each day I am grateful as we walk this journey together with the Lord. I love you.

ENRICO FABRIZI - Thank you for your continued help and support. Thank you for your guidance and assistance in my leadership and with this project. You continue to be a great leader, teacher, listener, advocate, friend, and supporter, investing in the lives of many people.

RICHARD PAUL LILLY - I'm glad we had the opportunity to work together on this project. Thank you for sharing your creative talent. The illustrations are beautifully done. Thank you for your assistance throughout.

FINALLY, I AM THANKFUL TO THE LORD for His faithfulness and great love each day and His continued guidance throughout this journey.

"Do not be anxious about anything, but in everything, by prayer and petition, with thanksgiving, present your requests to God. And the peace of God, which transcends all understanding, will guard your hearts and your minds in Christ Jesus."

–*Philippians 4:6-7 (NIV)*

www.mascotbooks.com

Cast Your Cares

For more information, please contact:
Mascot Books
620 Herndon Parkway #320
Herndon, VA 20170
info@mascotbooks.com

Library of Congress Control Number: 2018906444

CPSIA Code: PRT0818A
ISBN-13: 978-1-68401-906-9

Printed in the United States

CAST YOUR
Cares

Kristina Gipe
illustrated by Richard Paul Lilly

AT TIMES IN LIFE we may be scared,
but with the Lord by our side we can always be prepared.

We can take to God that which we fear,
and trust that He will hear and be near.

There are things in life that may
make us anxious, scared, or sad,
but having faith in God can help
us be glad.

The desires of our heart will be met in Him,
we should not allow things to block this
truth and cause us to sin.

THERE MAY BE TIMES
when others do not agree with
what we are trying to do,
but by committing our plans
to the Lord, we trust He
will guide our paths and see
us through.

When bad times come we
can always push ahead
and trust our lives
to the Lord and
look at what
His Word
has said.

Although things may work out different than we thought they would, faith in God through each step allows our hearts and minds to know things are working out as they should.

This can return our peace and joy to us, taking away our need to fuss.

THE PLANS HE HAS for us are
sometimes different than we think they should be,
    but faith tells us to trust in God for what we cannot see.

Knowing in our hearts that what His Word has said is true,
    and He has greater plans for us and will see us through.

The troubles of each day may at times make me feel down,
    but trusting in the Lord's love and care can turn all that around.

Let us look to the Lord in our time of need,
    as He will always help when we seek Him to lead.

Our Lord is always there to guide
    and will forever be by our side.

WE MAY NOT always understand why things happen the way they do,
but by faith we can believe the Lord will help see us through.

Although we cannot see God by faith we know He is always there,
His great love will surround us and we can take to Him every need and care.

Trusting God with all our needs will help us get through the day
and can give us peace and joy in everything we do and say.

At any time of the day we can always talk to God through prayer,
and know He's a loving Father who will guide and always be there.

JESUS TOOK QUIET TIME to be in prayer with His Father above, by doing the same we can be rested and refreshed in His great love.

Let us take His example and take time before God to be quiet and still, in doing this we can enjoy time with Him and learn His Will.

The stillness of our hearts and minds
can lead to greater rest,
    so each day we can be our very best!

Faith gives us hope in all that God can do,
    and we can know in our hearts and minds
    He will see us through.

SEEKING WHAT THE LORD
would like will lead me in His way,
and will take my mind off anxious
thoughts that might not make my day.

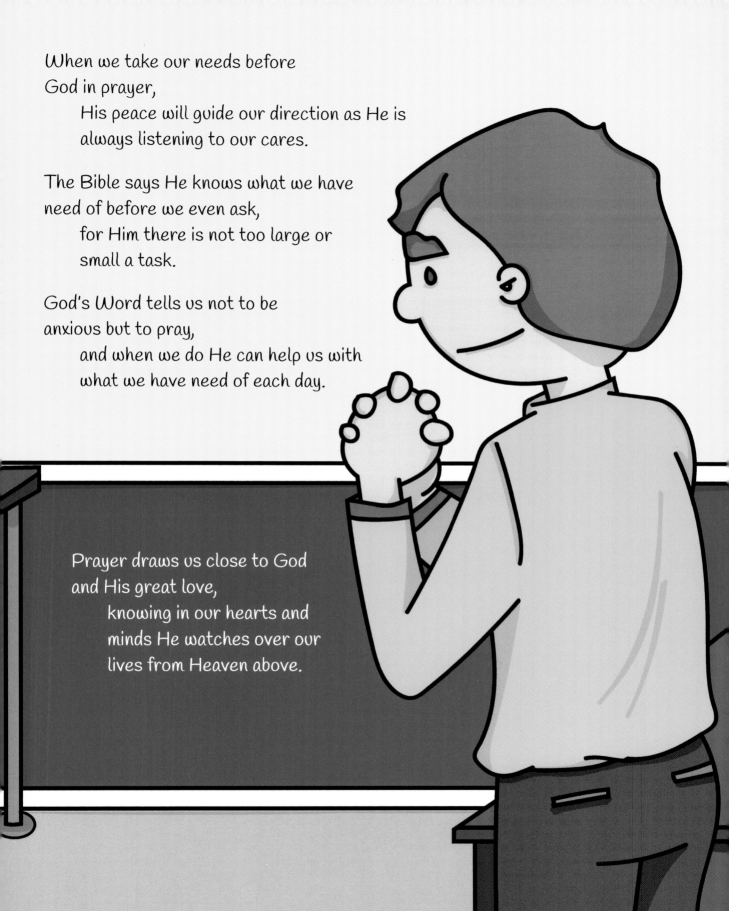

When we take our needs before
God in prayer,
     His peace will guide our direction as He is
     always listening to our cares.

The Bible says He knows what we have
need of before we even ask,
     for Him there is not too large or
     small a task.

God's Word tells us not to be
anxious but to pray,
     and when we do He can help us with
     what we have need of each day.

Prayer draws us close to God
and His great love,
     knowing in our hearts and
     minds He watches over our
     lives from Heaven above.

LIKE A SHEPHERD who protects the sheep,
He will protect those who of Him seek.

Our trust can be placed in all God can do,
and the fact that He will help see us through.

LET US GIVE HIM thanks and praise
and take in His unfailing love all of our days.

When we give thanks to God about all the ways
He's been there for us,
our hearts and minds can be free from
worry or fear because in Him we trust.

WE CAN BE GRATEFUL
for all that He has done,
knowing His love is so great
He sent His one and only Son.

Jesus Christ gave His life
upon the cross,
so we would be saved and
not be lost.

WITH GOD going before us He can make our paths straight,
and the peace within our hearts and minds will be great.

He wraps His arms around us when the days we face are tough,
and will hold on tightly to us, as His unfailing love is always enough.

We can take in His great peace each day,
knowing He goes before us and guides us in the right way.

JESUS SOUGHT the Lord in all that
He went through,
    the Father gave Him strength in all
    that He was given to do.

God gives us the best gift of
eternal life with Him,
    when we put our faith and trust in
    Jesus Christ who out of His great
    love on the cross wiped away our sin.

Faith allows us to gain trust in the Lord and
that He has great things in store for us,
    through this we can have confidence
    in God and always in Him trust.

Each day the Lord desires to bless us
with His great love,
    and watches over our lives
    from Heaven above.

GOD'S GREAT LOVE refreshes us each day,
   and allows us to grow in our lives in what we do and say.

Faith in God allows us to believe God's Word is true
   and that His love will surround and guide us through.

Faith says Jesus died for us to wash away our sins,
   preparing a great place for us in Heaven for eternity,
   and that He will come again!

ABOUT THE AUTHOR

KRISTINA GIPE received her bachelor's degree in Business, Management, and Economics with a concentration in Business Administration from Empire State College. The Lord placed it on her heart to write her first book, *15 Days of Love,* where she began her journey and found an undiscovered passion for writing. The Lord inspires Kristina every day to grow in faith and love, learning how to cast her cares.

www.walkinfaithlivebylove.com

Walk in Faith Live by Love